My Painted House,

My Friendly Chicken,

and Me

by Maya Angelou

Photographs by
Margaret Courtney-Clarke

Designed by
Alexander Isley Design

Clarkson Potter, Inc./Publishers
New York

Published by Clarkson N. Potter, Inc.,
201 East 50th Street, New York, New York 10022.
Member of the Crown Publishing Group.

Random House, Inc.
New York, Toronto, London, Sydney, Auckland
http://www.randomhouse.com/

Originally published in hardcover in 1994 by
Clarkson Potter/Publishers.

CLARKSON POTTER, POTTER, and colophon are
trademarks of Clarkson N. Potter, Inc.

Printed in Hong Kong

Library of Congress Cataloging-in-Publication Data
Angelou, Maya
My painted house, my friendly chicken, and me/ by Maya
Angelou; photographs by Margaret Courtney-Clarke.—
1st paperback ed.
1. Women, Ndebele—juvenile literature. [1. Art,
Ndebele—juvenile literature. 2. South Africa—Social life
and customs—juvenile literature.] I. Courtney-Clarke,
Margaret—ill. II. Title.
DT2913.N44A54   1994
704'.042'0968295—dc20   93-45735

ISBN 0-517-88815-7

10 9 8 7 6 5 4 3 2 1

First Paperback Edition

To all the children,
for they are
the hope of humankind.

Hello Stranger-friend.

I am Thandi, an Ndebele girl in South Africa.

I am eight years old, and my best friend

is a chicken.

You may laugh at that,

but when I tell my friend secrets, she can talk all she wants...but no one can understand her...except another chicken, of course. My chicken not only listens to my stories; she has other uses. If you play with her and take her mind off what's going on, you can quickly— very quickly—snatch a feather or two when she is distracted. She doesn't notice, and the feathers will come in handy later, of course.

I have two hopes. One is my name, Thandi

All children are hope for their families,
and many Ndebele girls are named Hope.
If you like, you can call yourself Hope, too.
In secret, of course.

Especially if you are a boy, of course.

which means hope in my language.

The other hope I have is that
at the end of this book I can say
"Good-bye friend," not
"Good-bye stranger-friend."

I don't know why, but Ndebele people do not call anything beautiful. They will say that the best thing is good. All Ndebele women paint their houses, and I want you to know, stranger-friend, no one's house is as good as my mother's. She has started to teach me to paint good, very good designs.

When I am
taller, I shall
have a house so
good people
will stop in
front of my
walls and smile,
and even laugh
out loud.

You have to
have strong
eyes to paint
good, and
your hand
must not
shake like a
leaf on a tree,
for you must
fill a chicken's
feather with
paint and
draw a line as
straight as a
spear.

You must have the

pattern inside your head,

even before you dip the

feather into the paint.

Your hand must be

steady to make the

patterns sharp,

the walls are high.

and your legs must be strong, because sometimes

My mother and her sisters sit by the fire in winter, or in summer under shade trees, and they make good things with beads.

They tell stories as they sort and string and sew. My mother lets me watch her and very soon I shall be making the *amaphotho* (a beaded apron) and the *ghabi* (the fringed loin flap), and they will be so good that when I dance, the stars will dance with me.

My father built us small houses,

and my mother painted them.

We pretend that we can

become small and go

inside and have our meal.

In my village,
the children
play with
penny
whistles

and b i c y c l e s .

Some are so shy
they try to lose
themselves in their
mothers' blankets,

and some just sit back deep inside themselve

nd look out at the world.

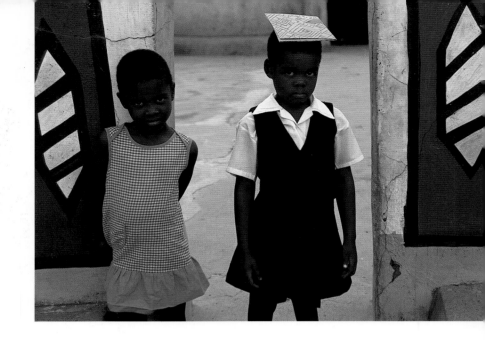

When my friends and I go to school, we wear th

uniforms Father bought in the town,

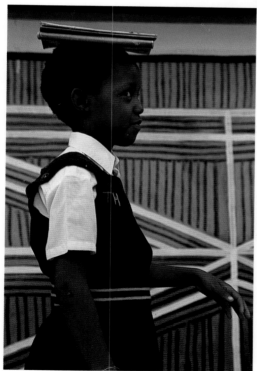

but when we
we start jumping
because we can
off those dry
clothes and pu
our beads agai
look

come home,
and laughing

take
dull
on
and

very good.

Sometimes I go to the city with my mother and

The women wear
their best blankets
and best neck rings
and very good leg
rings, of course.

sisters and aunts in a wagon pulled by four mules.

I am always happy to see
the city people stare at my
mother and relatives because
the city folk have nothing so
good as the Ndebele women.
Their houses are all one sad
color and the women I see
have no beads at all. I feel
sorry for them, and I give
them a good smile. It must
help because they laugh.

I wonder,

are little brothers in your village as **mischievous**

as my

little brother?

He wears a sun cap because he is supposed to tend sheep, but he is so mischievous that sometimes I would like to give him away,

to someone far, far away....

To a good person, of course. He tries to get into everybody's business, and even wants to make a chicken *his* best friend. He will never succeed. Mainly because you have to know how to speak to animals. My brother can't help SHOUTING, and of course the chicken runs away.

Now, about my very friend, the chicken.

She runs from me
only when she is on
her own errands,
but when she is free,
I take her in my arms
and tell her that I...

No. I can't tell you because you are not a chicken.

I have enjoyed telling you

my mother, and

the beads and the painted

the chicken. You may call me

to call you friend.

you hold my chicken.

about my village,

my squirmy brother,

houses, and my good friend,

friend, and I would like

f we ever meet, I will let

She will keep your secrets safe.

You know why, of course.